MAKING THE TEAM

· *Louanne Pig in* ·

MAKING THE TEAM

Nancy Carlson

PUFFIN BOOKS

PUFFIN BOOKS

A Division of Penguin Books USA Inc.
375 Hudson Street   New York, New York 10014
Penguin Books Ltd, Harmondsworth, Middlesex, England
Penguin Books Australia Ltd, Ringwood, Victoria, Australia
Penguin Books Canada Limited, 2801 John Street, Markham, Ontario, Canada L3R 1B4
Penguin Books (N.Z.) Ltd, 182–190 Wairau Road, Auckland 10, New Zealand

First published by Carolrhoda Books, Inc. , 1985
Published in Picture Puffins 1986
10 9 8 7 6 5 4 3
Copyright © Nancy Carlson, 1985
All rights reserved
Printed in USA
Set in Goudy Old Style

Library of Congress Cataloging in Publication Data
Carlson, Nancy L.   Louanne Pig in making the team.
Summary: Though she plans to try out for cheerleading, Louanne Pig helps
her friend Arnie try out for football, with surprising results.
[1. Sex role—Fiction.   2. Pigs—Fiction.   3. Football—Fiction]   I. Title.
PZ7.C21665Lj   1986   [E]   85-43263   ISBN 0-14-050601-2

This book is dedicated
to the memory of my dog,
Dame — my best pal. I miss her.

One day Louanne and Arnie found something exciting on the school bulletin board. Tryouts for the cheerleading squad and the football team were coming up.

"I'm going to try out for cheerleading," said Louanne.

"And I'm going to try out for the football team," said Arnie.

That afternoon they hurried over to Arnie's
to practice together.

Louanne was doing pretty well...

...until she came to the split jump. She couldn't get off the ground.

"Like this, Louanne," said Arnie.

"I'm better at cartwheels," said Louanne.

"Let me show you how to do it," said Arnie.

"You ought to be practicing football," said Louanne, and she picked up the football and threw it to Arnie.

Arnie missed the catch.

"You have to keep your eye on the ball,
Arnie," Louanne told him. "Like this."

"I'm probably better at tackling," said Arnie.

"Let me show you how to do it," said
Louanne.

"Let's try some kicking," said Arnie.

All week long Louanne and Arnie met after school to practice for their tryouts. Louanne's jumps didn't improve much, but Arnie kept her spirits up.

"You really look great!" he told her.

Arnie only rarely caught the ball, but Louanne encouraged him.

"I know you're going to make the team!" she said.

When the big day arrived, their confidence
was high.

Cheerleading tryouts were first.

Louanne didn't make the squad.
"Don't feel bad," Arnie consoled her. "There's always next year. By then you'll be top-notch."

"Right," said Louanne. "Come on. There's still a little time before your tryout. I'll show you a few last tricks."

"Hey, pig," said Coach Ed. "You're pretty good. Why don't you try out for the team."

So Louanne and Arnie tried out together.
Louanne made the team.

Arnie didn't.

Suddenly Louanne had an idea.
"Come on, Arnie!" she said. "Cheerleading tryouts are still going on."

That fall Roosevelt School won every game.
Louanne led the team to victory,

and Arnie led the cheers.